TEMPEST TERROR!

ROSS MONTGOMERY

With illustrations by

Mark Beech

Barrington Stoke

First published in 2021 in Great Britain by
Barrington Stoke Ltd
18 Walker Street, Edinburgh, EH3 7LP

www.barringtonstoke.co.uk

A CIP catalogue record for this book is available from the British Library upon request

ISBN: 978-1-78112-961-6

Printed by Hussar Books, Poland

To all the hardworking teachers and teaching assistants – well done for keeping it together while we navigate this brave new world

CONTENTS

CHAPTER 1

The Storm

CRAAASH!

We held on tight to the tiny life raft as the storm swept around us. Our clothes were soaking and our hair was dripping wet as the waves shook our boat like an angry monster. Through the howling wind and rain, I could just make out our ferry as it sank into the sea. I closed my eyes, gripped the side of the boat and prayed.

It wasn't supposed to be like this. My drama club were supposed to be heading to a Shakespeare festival in Italy to perform *The Tempest*, the play we'd spent all last term working on. It was supposed to be the trip of a lifetime, but the second we stepped onto the ferry that morning, I knew that something was wrong.

Our headmaster, Mr Fortune, had booked the cheapest tickets he could find. The ferry looked like it was held together with old plasters and chewing gum! How was this heap of junk supposed to get us all the way to Italy?

Well, it didn't. Only an hour after we left the port, a huge storm blew up out of nowhere. It tossed our rickety ship around like an old shoebox and made it capsize in minutes. Everyone had to abandon ship and scramble into life rafts as the storm grew worse and worse around us. Our dream trip had turned into a disaster!

Mr Fortune stood at the front of our life raft waving a clipboard over his head.

"Don't panic, children!" he shouted. "It's just a small hitch! Listen carefully while I check everyone's here – Blake? Dom? Ruby? Claire? Steve? Rianna? Frank?"

One by one, the others shouted, "Here!" My name was last, as always. To be honest, I'm amazed Mr Fortune even remembered me.

"See? Everyone's safe!" said Mr Fortune, trying to sound cheerful. "Your other classmates are on the life raft just behind us. So long as you stay sitting down and keep your life jackets on, you'll all be perfectly—"

"LOOK OUT!" shouted Ruby.

SPLASH!

Before Mr Fortune could finish his sentence, a huge wave swept over the boat and sent him reeling into the water. He hadn't been sitting down *or* wearing his life jacket, of course. Mr Fortune waved his hands above his head for a moment, then another wave sloshed over him and he sank from sight. We all screamed.

"Mr Fortune!" cried Dom. "Come back!"

"You've got my asthma inhaler!" wailed Claire.

Blake pointed at something in the distance. "Er ... guys? What *is* that?"

I turned around – and my stomach dropped. Another wave was heading right for us – but this one was the size of a cliff face. There was no way our life raft would survive it.

"HOLD ON, EVERYONE!" screamed Ruby.

I screwed my eyes shut, held on tight as the boat turned upside down ... and then there was nothing but darkness.

CHAPTER 2

The Island

I was having the most wonderful dream.

I was lying on a hot sandy beach, with the sun warming my skin and the waves lapping at my toes.

This is the life, I thought.

Then I felt a crab scuttle over my face.

Wow, I thought. *This dream is pretty realistic ... OW!*

I sat up. I really *did* have a crab on my face, and it had just pinched my nose. I had seaweed in my glasses too, and sand in my mouth. What was going on?

I looked around in amazement. This was no dream. I really *was* lying on a sandy beach. That really *was* the ocean, sparkling in the midday sun in front of me. I could even see a forest of palm trees swaying in the distance. How did I end up here?

Then it all came back to me. The storm, the ferry sinking, Mr Fortune falling in the water, the huge wave heading towards us ...

I couldn't believe it. I was shipwrecked on a desert island! But where were the others?

That's when I saw them, sitting sadly under the palm trees. They all looked soaking wet and miserable. There was Dom and Ruby and Claire and Steve and Rianna ... but that was it. I couldn't see Mr Fortune, or anyone from the other lifeboat. Half the kids from our school trip were missing.

I stood up slowly and went to join the others. Ruby saw me first and pointed. "Everyone – look! Someone's washed up!"

Dom jumped to his feet. "Who is it?"

Steve looked up and muttered, "No one – just Frank."

Everyone groaned, disappointed that it was me. I should have been offended, but to be honest I wasn't even surprised. That's just how things have always been for me at school.

I'm the kind of person who fades into the background – Mr Sensible, quiet and dull.

Then last summer, I got a part in my school's production of Shakespeare's *A Midsummer Night's Dream* and got bitten by the acting bug.

I thought I'd *hate* being in the spotlight, but the moment I stepped onto the stage I felt full of confidence. I loved being the centre of attention! When I heard that the school drama club was putting on a production of another Shakespeare play called *The Tempest,* I signed up straight away. So long, Mr Sensible!

But the moment I got to rehearsals I felt like I was out of my depth. The rest of the drama club were ten times more confident than me: they had bigger voices and better ideas and were much more used to being in the spotlight. Once they started speaking, I couldn't get a word in.

I was given the smallest part in the play – Francisco, who only says about ten lines – and I spent most of my time on stage hidden behind the others. All my new-found confidence vanished – I hardly even talked during rehearsals. No wonder no one had even noticed that I was missing.

"Some trip this is," muttered Ruby, who was always complaining. "We'll never get to the Globe-Trotters International Shakespeare Festival now."

I gulped. Not making the festival was the least of our worries. We were stranded on a desert island! Without an adult to help us, we were just six kids stuck in the middle of nowhere.

Then I realised – there were only six of us. There should have been seven. Mr Fortune wasn't the only one missing from our life raft.

"Where's Blake?" I asked.

There was a nasty silence, and everyone looked at their feet. I knew what that meant – Blake was missing too.

No wonder everyone looked so upset. Blake was the most popular kid in school, with the best hair and the coolest clothes. Whenever he talked – no matter how boring it was – people listened. He'd got the part of the main romantic lead in our play: dashing young Ferdinand. It didn't seem to bother anyone that he couldn't act.

"I can't take this any more!" said Dom. "We can't just sit here! We have to find Blake!"

Dom was Blake's best friend, but sometimes he was more like Blake's devoted puppy. Dom had even made sure he got the part of Ferdinand's father, King Alonso, so he and Blake could hang out together in rehearsals.

"Are you crazy?" snapped Ruby. "We can't go looking for him just because he's your friend! We have to stay here and wait for someone to save us!"

Ruby was always arguing with Dom. Everyone knew that it was because *she'd* wanted the part of King Alonso, but Mr Fortune had made her the evil Antonio instead. She was clearly still annoyed about it.

"Then we should phone someone for help!" said Dom.

Ruby shook her head. "Mr Fortune has all our phones. We should stay here, where we know it's safe."

"That's right!" cried Claire. "This island could be swarming with diseases!"

Claire was Ruby's friend, and a total clean freak – her clothes were always brand new and her hair was always perfect. People swore they'd even seen her ironing her script once. She played the part of Sebastian, King Alonso's evil brother.

"But what about food?" groaned Steve, his stomach growling. "We could starve to death before anyone shows up to save us! There was hardly anything to eat in those ferry vending machines."

Steve was always hungry – he was always scoffing biscuits or trying to microwave some chips in rehearsals. He was the class joker, which was why he was given the part of Stephano, who was the clown of the play.

"Does anyone have any better ideas?" snapped Ruby.

I looked around. There was one other person left – Rianna, silent as always. She'd been given the role of Adrian, another small part with just a few lines like me. We should have had lots in common, seeing as all our scenes were together, but we never spoke. She had joined our school at the beginning of term and almost never said a word. I hardly knew anything about her.

Meanwhile, Dom was stamping his foot. "Shut up! *I'm* in charge, and I say we go looking for Blake!"

Ruby frowned. "Who made *you* boss?"

"I'm the oldest," said Dom. "And I have the most important part in the play out of everyone here. That makes me the leader!"

"That's not fair!" cried Steve.

They all started fighting. I sighed – they were always doing that. At every rehearsal one of them would start an argument, and Mr Fortune would have to step in and calm everyone down. But of course, Mr Fortune wasn't here any more.

Things were getting worse by the second. We had no food, no water, no idea how long it would be before someone found us, and now no one could agree on anything. It was going to get dark soon too.

"Er ... maybe we should split up and search the island?" I said.

No one heard me – they were all too busy arguing. It was just like rehearsals all over again. What a bunch of drama queens! I coughed.

"I said, maybe we should split up and search the island? The others might have washed up somewhere else. One group could look for them, and another group could look for food or water."

Something very strange happened. Dom had been watching me talk out of the corner of his eye – then he clicked his fingers and turned to the others.

"Right – change of plan!" he said. "I've just had a brilliant idea. Let's split up and search the island!"

Everyone muttered in agreement. Dom had just stolen my idea! I was so annoyed, my glasses steamed up. Dom went on handing out orders.

"Ruby and Claire – you look for water. Steve – you look for food. I'll go and find Blake!"

"What about Mr Fortune and the others?" Ruby asked.

"Yeah, you can look for them too," said Dom with a shrug. "Everyone meet back here in one hour!"

With that, they strolled off in their separate directions. I stood up, confused.

"Er ... what about me and Rianna?" I asked. "What should *we* do?"

Dom glanced over his shoulder. "Oh – I dunno. Stay here and keep an eye on stuff, I guess."

I frowned. "Keep an eye on what – the sand?"

But Dom wasn't even listening. He marched away down the beach, off to find his friend. Rianna and I were left all alone.

My glasses steamed up again. No one listened to me at school – and it looked like no one was going to listen to me here, either.

Even on a desert island, some things never change.

CHAPTER 3

Be Not Afeard

I sat down on the sand and let out another deep sigh. I guess waiting on the beach wasn't so bad. After all, the island was beautiful. The sea was sparkling and the trees were swaying in the breeze. Everything was calm and quiet ...

"That was a good idea," said a voice behind me.

I almost jumped ten feet in the air. I'd completely forgotten that Rianna was with me too. The last thing I expected was for her to start talking!

"W-what was a good idea?" I asked.

"Splitting up and searching the island," said Rianna. "I heard you say it first. It was good of you to let Dom take the credit."

I blushed. "Well, it was the sensible thing to do. The last thing we need right now is more arguing."

Rianna nodded. "Us sensible people don't normally get a word in, do we? Not with people like Dom and Ruby taking centre stage."

I was amazed. It was the most I'd ever heard Rianna say in one go. She wasn't silent after all – maybe she was just more comfortable talking away from a large group.

"Funny, isn't it?" she said. "A storm that came out of nowhere? Getting stranded on a desert island?"

She waited for me to get the joke, but I didn't laugh. It didn't seem very funny to me. She gave a sigh.

"Don't you see? It's exactly what happens in *The Tempest*!"

I gasped – Rianna was right. I'd been so busy worrying about what had happened to us that I hadn't even noticed that it was exactly like our play!

The Tempest is about an old wizard named Prospero, who lives on a magical island with his daughter, Miranda. He also has two servants: a fairy named Ariel and a fish-like monster called Caliban. Prospero used to be a powerful duke, but his evil brother, Antonio, stole his title and sent him off to sea in a rotten boat, expecting him to die. Prospero survived, but he was stuck on a desert island with no hope of ever getting home.

Then one day, by chance, Prospero sees evil Antonio sailing past the island on a boat with King Alonso, his son Prince Ferdinand and some noblemen. It's his chance for revenge! First, he gets his fairy servant Ariel to create a magical storm that shipwrecks everyone on the island. Then he splits them up into different groups.

Everyone thinks that Ferdinand has drowned, but really he's just washed up on the other side of the island. Now Prospero can set up his daughter, Miranda, with the dashing young prince.

Meanwhile, the evil Antonio is plotting to kill King Alonso so that Alonso's brother can be king with him, Antonio, as his sidekick. Prospero uses magic and trickery to ruin their plan and at the end of the play he shows everyone the truth about Antonio's wicked ways!

It's a classic Shakespeare happy ending. By the close of the play, Ferdinand and Miranda are going to get married, King Alonso has got his son back, the baddies have all been punished, Ariel and Caliban have won their freedom, and everyone leaves the island happy!

Rianna was right – what had happened to us so far was exactly like the play. A storm, a shipwreck, a desert island ... and now Blake was missing too, just like Ferdinand!

"It's a coincidence," I said.

Rianna looked at me. "Really? A coincidence? Look over there and tell me what you see!"

She pointed at the forest behind us. It was beautiful. Beneath every palm tree were clusters of flowers, bristling cacti, creeping vines, and leaves in a hundred different colours.

"A forest?" I said.

"A *tropical* forest," said Rianna. "We were only on that ferry for an hour before the storm hit. How many tropical islands do you know that are a few miles off the coast of Dover?"

I was speechless. I'd been wrong about Rianna. She was smart. Just because she was quiet, it didn't mean she had nothing to say.

"And you know what else is weird?" she went on. "It's not just Blake and Mr Fortune and the rest of the drama club who are missing. Where are the other passengers from the ferry? Where are the staff? Not one of them has washed up on the beach with us. It's like we've been transported to the other side of the world!"

I shook my head. Time to be Mr Sensible again. "Rianna, I know it's a strange situation, but there's got to be a perfectly good explanation for—"

Rianna shoved her hand over my mouth. "Shhh! Do you hear that?"

And then I heard it. Music. And not just any music – *beautiful* music. It unspooled between the trees like golden ribbon, rising and falling on the wind ...

"Music in the trees!" Rianna whispered. "Just like in the play!"

She stopped to think for a moment, and then she started to recite one of the poems from the play, word-perfect:

Be not afeard. The isle is full of noises,

Sounds, and sweet airs that give delight and

hurt not ...

I gasped. She was right – in *The Tempest*, the island is filled with invisible spirits who make beautiful magical music!

Just as suddenly as it had started, the music stopped and the beach fell silent. Rianna stared at me in amazement.

"How can you explain that, Frank? Something really strange is going on here! Maybe that was no ordinary storm. Maybe it was a *magical* storm – a magical storm that's taken us into *The Tempest* for real!"

I couldn't help myself. I stared at Rianna for a moment ... and then burst out laughing.

"Rianna, listen to yourself!" I said. "You can't get a ferry into a Shakespeare play!"

Rianna frowned. "How else can you explain what's happened?"

"Who knows?" I laughed. "Maybe Mr Fortune and Blake haven't disappeared after all. Maybe they were eaten by a monster like Caliban ..."

I was cut short by another sound in the trees – but it wasn't more beautiful music.

This time, it was a scream.

Rianna and I jumped up fast just as Steve came crashing out of the forest. He was covered in cuts and broken twigs – and he looked absolutely terrified.

"Quick! It's coming! Run for your lives!"

Rianna and I were confused. *What* was coming?

By now the others had heard the scream and come running back too. They were all staring at Steve, who was still screaming and talking nonsense. Dom took charge, grabbed Steve and shook him hard.

"Calm down!" he shouted. "For goodness' sake – what happened? Did you find Blake?"

The words all came spilling out of Steve at once. "N-no! I – I was looking for food just like you said, and then suddenly I heard this beautiful music playing in the trees—"

"We heard that too!" said Ruby and Claire.

Steve nodded fast. "So ... so I went to see where it was coming from, and I found ... I found ..."

Dom lost his patience. “Spit it out! What did you find?”

“A MONSTER!”

Everyone froze. Steve pointed at the trees, his eyes bugging out of his head.

“I mean it!” he said. “I saw it with my own eyes! A huge clumsy monster that stank of fish!”

Rianna and I stared at each other. It couldn’t be true – it *couldn’t*. But we only needed to take one look at Steve’s face to see that he wasn’t lying. He was terrified.

“That’s right,” he said. “It was a monster that stank of fish. Just like Caliban. Just like the monster in *The Tempest*!”

CHAPTER 4

Strange Bedfellows

Our group was silent with shock. We weren't just shipwrecked any more – now we were marooned with a monster!

"You – you must have made a mistake," said Dom, his voice shaking. "I didn't hear any music. Maybe you've got a bit of sunstroke and imagined the whole thing! It – it must have been Leo that you saw. That's it! He must have washed up on the island too and come looking for us!"

Leo was the boy who played Caliban in our school production – he'd been on the other life raft, along with the actors who played Prospero, Ariel and Miranda.

"What – he came looking for us dressed in his costume?!" snorted Ruby. "Don't be an idiot, Dom. You heard what Steve said – it was a huge, hairy monster that stank of fish! Does that sound like Leo to you?"

Everyone thought about it.

"Well, I guess he's not *that* hairy," said Ruby.

"It wasn't Leo!" Steve went on. "It was much, much bigger than him! And it didn't sound like him either; it made an animal noise! I'm telling you, there's a monster on this island!"

I glanced at Rianna – the look she gave me said it all. Everything that she had said was coming true. Meanwhile, Dom looked terrified too. The news that his beloved Blake could be gobbled up by a monster was too much for him to take.

“R-rubbish!” he said. “You’re making it up. Come on, quit messing around and let’s look for Blake ...”

“But what about Mr Fortune and the others?” said Steve. “We have to find them before Caliban gets them too!”

“Forget the others!” said Ruby. “We need to stay here, where the monster can’t get *us*!”

“THERE – IS – NO – MONSTER!” cried Dom. “I’m leader and I say we go and find Blake, right now!”

In two seconds flat, they were all arguing again. Rianna and I looked at each other – this was the last thing we needed. She coughed and stepped forward.

"Look – it's going to get dark soon," she said. "Before we do anything else, we need to make sure we have a shelter and a fire – if not, we'll freeze to death once the sun goes down ..."

No one was listening to her, as usual – except for Dom, who was glancing at her out of the corner of his eye. He stamped his foot.

"Right! Change of plan," he barked. "Forget searching the island – we need to make a shelter and a fire, right now!"

Rianna's face fell. Dom had just pulled the same dirty trick that he'd pulled on me! Once again, he started to hand out orders.

"Steve! You collect firewood. Ruby and Claire! You search the beach for anything we can use as shelter. I'll stay here and dig a big manly firepit, seeing as I'm the leader."

He was trying to sound like he was still in charge, but it wasn't working any more. Everyone could see that he was trying to hide how frightened he was. Ruby and Claire gave each other a look behind his back.

"Really?" said Ruby. "You're sure you don't want to keep looking for Blake on your own?"

Dom looked like he might be sick. "N-no! If we build a big enough fire, Blake will be able to find us! Now what did I say? Everyone GO!"

The others grumbled and left to do their jobs. Once again, Dom hadn't given Rianna or me anything to do.

"He's such a jerk," I whispered to her. "I heard what you said – it was all your idea, not Dom's."

"I know," she muttered. "Come on – let's help Steve get some firewood. We're going to need as much as we can to make it through the night."

I frowned. "You – you don't think what Steve said was true, do you? About Caliban?"

Rianna gave me a worried look. “I don’t know. But we’d better get that shelter made fast—”

“Pssst!”

We spun round. Ruby and Claire were standing right behind us, smiling warmly.

“Fred, Diana – how’s it going?”

My glasses steamed up. “It’s Frank and Rianna.”

“Whatever,” said Ruby. She leaned forward, her voice low and dangerous. “Claire and I have been talking, and we don’t think Dom is fit to be leader any more. If he stays in charge, all he’s going to do is make us look for Blake! Caliban will eat us all before morning!”

“If we don’t all catch salmonella first,” moaned Claire.

Ruby nodded. "We need a new leader. Someone clever and quick. Someone who's brave and bold with good posture and really good hair."

She tossed her hair back. I gasped – so that was Ruby's plan. She wanted to get rid of Dom and put herself in charge!

"What do you say?" said Claire. "Are you on our side or not?"

I looked at them nervously. Ruby and Claire were both a hundred times more confident than me – they always got their way. But I had to speak out.

"I … I think it's a bad idea," I said softly. "We all want to get home. We should focus on working together and not argue about who gets to be in charge."

"He's right," said Rianna. "And you two need to build that shelter, fast, or else we're all in trouble!"

You could have heard a pin drop. Ruby and Claire looked at each other.

"Have it your way, Diana," said Ruby coldly.

With that, they stormed away. I gulped. "That didn't sound good," I said.

Rianna made a face. "Please! Ruby's all talk. Trust me – once the shelter's built and we've got a proper fire going, things will calm down again."

But we got a nasty shock when we returned to camp. The others might be good actors, but they were terrible campers. Ruby and Claire's shelter was a few scrappy branches leaning against each other – they looked as if they'd collapse in the softest breeze. Dom's firepit was an enormous soggy hole with a pool of seawater at the bottom.

"We can't light a fire in there," I said. "It's too damp!"

“Rubbish!” said Dom. “It’ll dry out once the fire’s started. Anyone got any matches?”

Everyone stared at him. Dom’s face fell. No one had thought about how to start the fire! The sun was already setting and soon it was going to get dark.

Ruby gave a mean grin. "Any more great ideas, Dom? Without a fire, we're going to freeze to death!"

She was right – our clothes were still damp from the storm. Now it was getting dark I was already starting to shiver.

Dom frowned. "I ... er ... well ..."

"Everyone! Look what I just found!"

We turned around. Steve was dragging a giant wheelie suitcase towards us.

"It's one of Mr Fortune's suitcases!" he said. "It just washed up on the beach!"

Dom quickly took back control. "See? There's bound to be something in there we can use to start a fire!"

"Or our phones!" gasped Ruby.

"Or my asthma inhaler!" cried Claire.

"Or FOOD!" bellowed Steve, throwing the suitcase down beside us. "Delicious, wonderful food! Biscuits, chocolate, crisps ..."

He tore open the suitcase ... and everything fell out onto the sand at once. There were no phones or snacks inside. Instead, there was just ... the costumes from our play.

Dom picked up a frilly ruff. "Well, er ... at least we have some dry clothes, eh?" he said.

Ten minutes later, the six of us were wearing our stage costumes, squished under the shelter like Shakespearean sardines. Rianna and I both wore ruffs and britches. Steve wore his jester's costume, with his floppy hat and bells. Dom wore his king's robes and crown. Ruby and Claire were trying to keep warm under their big fake beards. We must have looked ridiculous – not that anyone else was here to see us. It was already pitch-dark and a cold wind howled over the island. The thought that there could be a monster out there hunting for us sent shivers up my spine.

"There!" said Dom. "Much better."

"Sure," muttered Ruby. "Maybe Caliban will be laughing too hard to eat us."

"There is no Caliban!" said Dom. "Stop frightening everyone."

"And stop talking about eating things!" Steve begged. "Please! I'm starving."

Steve wasn't the only one. None of us had eaten since breakfast. All our stomachs growled at the same time. I was so hungry I could barely think straight.

"There were hot dogs on the ferry," said Claire, drooling.

"I had biscuits in my backpack," sighed Rianna.

"I'd murder every single one of you for a packet of crisps," said Steve.

"Why bother?" said Ruby. "Caliban will murder us first."

"THERE – IS – NO – CALIBAN!" bellowed Dom. "Stop bleating on about monsters! We all need to focus on getting a good night's sleep so we can get up bright and early and start looking for Blake—"

That was too much for Ruby. She lost her temper. "For heaven's sake – Blake, Blake, Blake! You're like a stuck record!"

I groaned. I knew exactly where this was heading – yet another argument. It was the last thing we needed now everyone was hungry and frightened. But there was no stopping Ruby.

"Can't you face facts?" she went on. "Blake's not here! He's in the middle of the ocean with Mr Fortune and the others – if he hasn't been swallowed up by Caliban already! He's gone, finished, sea-swallowed, exit stage left ..."

“What are you talking about?” said a voice in the dark. “I’m right here.”

We all screamed, and the shelter collapsed. We crawled out from under the branches, groaning and confused, staring at the person sitting on the sand beside us.

It couldn’t be ... But it was. There was Blake, alive and well, playing on his phone as if it was the most normal thing in the world.

I couldn’t believe it – Blake was alive! And, as usual, playing on his phone. Even on a desert island, some things never change.

CHAPTER 5

The Banquet Vanishes

"Blake!" said Steve. "How long have you been sitting there?"

Blake shrugged. "Dunno – maybe ten minutes? You were all busy arguing, so I thought I'd wait out here until you were done."

Dom threw himself at Blake and tackled him to the ground. "Blake! Where have you been?" he wailed. "I thought Caliban had eaten you!"

Blake frowned. “What are you talking about? I’ve been on the other side of the island all day! I washed up there this morning.”

“What about Mr Fortune and the rest of the drama club?” asked Claire. “Did they wash up with you?”

Blake shook his head. “No. But I did find Mr Fortune’s bag with all our phones in it. I’ve been playing *Gore Quest* all day! It’s been brilliant.”

Rianna and I looked at each other. Blake might be the star performer of the play, but he wasn’t exactly the smartest guy in the world.

“What about the ... the monster?” asked Steve, trembling. “Did you see it?”

Blake thought about it. “A monster? Don’t think so. I’ve been too busy trying to beat my high score! I’m almost out of battery though, so I thought I’d come and find you all before ...”

Right on cue, his screen went blank.

"Oh, it's gone," he said. "Anyone got a charger?"

This was too much. Rianna lost her temper. "You idiot! You've had a phone all this time and you used it to play some stupid game?! We could have called for help or—"

"Wait," said Claire – cutting her off as usual. "What's that?"

She pointed to the spot where Blake was sitting. There, on the sand beside him, was an empty packet of crisps, a dozen chocolate wrappers and a bottle of cola.

"SNACKS!" Steve roared. "HE HAS SNACKS!"

He threw himself at Blake. We held him back as best we could, but it was hard work. Steve was all arms as he tried to grab Blake *and* any food that was left.

"Where did you get those treats?" gasped Claire.

Blake pointed down the beach. "There are boxes and boxes on the other side of the island! Crisps, sandwiches, cakes ... I just helped myself!"

Dom gasped. "They must have washed up from the ferry! Someone should go and get them!"

There was a very long, very loud silence. Everyone looked at each other.

"SOMEONE should go and get them," Dom said a second time.

"Why not you?" said Ruby. "You're our brave and fearless leader!"

Dom trembled. "I – I'm not hungry!"

Ruby laughed. "Ha! I knew it! You're frightened of Caliban!"

Dom glared at her. "YOU go and get them then, if you're so brave!"

They all started arguing – again. I groaned. There was no point in me and Rianna trying to stop them – Dom would just steal our ideas, if he listened to us at all. Besides, this argument sounded even worse than normal. It was time to be Mr Sensible again. There was something far more important than food on the other side of the island.

"Blake, do you remember where you left that bag of phones?" I asked.

Blake nodded. "Of course – I never forget a phone."

"Great! You can show us the way," said Rianna. "Hopefully one of them will still work and we can call for help before that lot kill each other. Honestly, they'd argue over the colour of the sky if you gave them a chance!"

I made a face. I was keen to get away from the argument, but getting the phones meant walking to the other side of the island. If what Steve had said was true, that meant we could come face to face with a terrible monster.

It sounded unlikely – but then, everything else from *The Tempest* had come true. The shipwreck, losing Blake, the music in the trees ... Blake said that he hadn't seen any monsters, but he was so obsessed with his phone he probably wouldn't have noticed if Caliban had spent all afternoon chewing on his leg.

We walked across the beach, and soon all the sounds of arguing were gone. The island was almost pitch-black – the only light came from the full moon that shone off the trees and made the sand as white as ground bones.

"Are we almost there?" I asked.

Blake pointed to the forest. "Nearly! I left the bag of phones in there, where I found the boxes of snacks. The food was stacked up under the trees!"

Rianna frowned. "But if they washed up on the beach, how did they get into the forest?"

Blake looked at her blankly. He definitely wasn't the right person to ask a question like that.

"Let's just grab the phones and get out of here," I muttered. "This place is giving me the creeps."

It was true. The wind roared across the sea and made the treetops shudder. We followed Blake into the gloomy forest until we came to a small clearing lit by moonlight. It was empty. Blake looked around, puzzled.

Rianna frowned. "Are you sure we're in the right place?"

"Of course!" said Blake. "The boxes were right here! There were loads of them – it's like they've all vanished into thin air!"

Rianna and I looked at each other. We didn't need words to know what the other was thinking. A feast that vanishes, as if by magic – that happens in *The Tempest* too.

Everything in the play was coming true, bit by bit. And that meant …

CRAAAAAAASH!

The trees at the edge of the forest were torn apart, and my blood froze in my veins. There, standing in the clearing in front of us, was a huge, hairy monster – a monster that stank of rotten fish.

It was Caliban. He was real – and he had found us.

CHAPTER 6

Caliban

We stared at the monster in horror. Caliban was just as awful as Steve had said ... no, he was *worse*. His body was covered in slimy rotten hair that hung in clumps from his face. He swayed to and fro as he came towards us, as if every step hurt him. He made low growling animal moans. I couldn't believe it. There really was a monster on this island!

Caliban gave another growl and turned his head. He still hadn't seen us! I swallowed down my fear.

"D-don't panic," I whispered. "Everyone stay as still as you can – if we don't move or make a sound, maybe Caliban won't be able to—"

"AAAAAARGH!" Blake yelled. "A MONSTER!"

He turned and fled, leaving Rianna and me by ourselves. Now Caliban knew *exactly* where we were. He turned to face us and charged with a terrible roar ...

"NO!"

Rianna leapt forward and gave Caliban a big push. The monster tripped backwards, lost his footing on a tree root ... and fell straight into a massive cactus patch. He gave an enormous bellow of pain and anger.

"RUN!" Rianna screamed as she grabbed my hand.

We tore out of the trees and back onto the beach, our feet flying over the sand as we followed Blake's footprints back to camp.

"That coward!" I panted. "I can't believe he just left us!"

"Can you blame him?" said Rianna, racing beside me. "That thing was awful – and those cacti won't stop it for long! We have to get back to the camp and warn the others!"

My heart pounded. She was right. It was only a matter of time before Caliban came after us. The camp was already close – I could hear Blake shouting to the others at the top of his lungs. At first I thought he was telling everyone about the monster ... but then I heard Dom shouting too.

"Help! Blake! Save me!"

I frowned. *Save me?* That didn't make any sense. What was going on?

Rianna and I got to the campsite ... and we saw what had happened while we were away.

Claire and Steve were holding back Blake as he tried to get away from them. They both had stage make-up smeared on their faces to look like warpaint.

"What are you doing?" Blake shouted. "Let Dom go!"

I gawped. Dom was tied to the nearest tree with his own stage stockings!

"Blake! Help me!" he screamed. "They said they're going to—"

Before he could finish his sentence, Ruby stuffed a ruff into his mouth and gagged him. She had covered her face in warpaint too, and was wearing Dom's crown and robes.

"Dom's not in charge any more – I am!" Ruby told us. "And my first act as leader is to feed the hungry beast of the island. We're offering him Dom as a sacrifice so Caliban will leave us alone! It's what the group wants!"

I could tell straight away that this wasn't true – Steve and Claire looked terrified. They'd only agreed with Ruby because they were afraid.

"How on earth did they do all of this so quickly?" muttered Rianna. "We've only been gone ten minutes."

I gritted my teeth. I didn't know the answer – but I knew that this had gone far enough. We didn't need any more arguments. We didn't need a leader who was going to string people up. What we needed was someone sensible.

And I'm Mr Sensible.

I drew a deep breath, planted my feet in the ground ... and shouted louder than I've ever shouted in my life.

"EVERYONE – LISTEN!"

The others all stopped arguing and turned to look at me. They had hardly heard me speak before, let alone shout.

"Caliban's coming this way. He's going to find us at any moment!"

Ruby gasped. "Quick, everyone! I'll prepare the sacrificial offering ..."

"NO!"

Everyone stopped again – and this time they turned to face Rianna. The look on their faces said it all – first Frank starts talking and now *her*?

"We're supposed to be a team!" said Rianna. "We're supposed to help each other. Do you think the monster will leave us alone after he's eaten Dom? Or will it be one of *you* next time, tied to that tree?"

Everyone was stunned – it was probably the most they'd ever heard Rianna say in one go.

"Then – what do we do?" said Steve.

There was a sudden sound from down the beach – the roar of the monster! Caliban was even closer than I had expected. Dom gave a muffled scream and fainted. The others panicked. There was nowhere for us to hide – if we ran into the trees, Caliban would pick us off one by one. All we had was a broken shelter and a damp firepit ...

I thought fast. "Rianna and Ruby, untie Dom! Everyone else, stand behind the firepit! No time to explain!"

Everyone did as they were told. Ruby and Rianna freed Dom and dragged him to the other side of the firepit. I could hear Caliban's horrible roar of pain getting louder and louder as he charged down the beach towards us ...

"We have to run!" cried Ruby. "We can't just stand here on the beach!"

"No one move!" I shouted. "We've only got one chance to get this right ..."

I ran over to the branches that had been our shelter and grabbed as many as I could. Then I threw them over the hole of the firepit, stood firm and faced the darkness.

There, standing on the beach ahead of us, was Caliban. He couldn't have been more than twenty feet away. I was completely terrified – but everyone was counting on me. I had to be brave. I gritted my teeth, took another breath and yelled as loud as I could.

"HEY, CALIBAN, OVER HERE!"

The monster spun round to face us. Then he gave a great roar and charged forward with his arms out ...

My plan worked perfectly. The monster ran straight over the branches I'd thrown on the sand and fell right into the enormous firepit hidden beneath them.

SQUELCH!

Caliban landed in the boggy pit, like a rock dropped in a well full of custard. He roared as he tried to pull himself free, but he was stuck fast.

"Phew! Sorry, everyone," I said. "I didn't have time to explain – I had to use us as bait so Caliban would fall in the pit!"

"We were BAIT?!" snapped Ruby.

But the others were amazed.

"Frank – you're a genius!" said Rianna.

"You captured the monster!" cried Steve.

"Frank the Caliban Killer!" cried Claire.

I was surprised myself. Who would have thought that I – Frank, Mr Sensible – could take charge in a crisis and save everyone from a monster attack? I had to admit, Frank the Caliban Killer had quite a nice ring to it ...

"Er ... is that *really* a monster?" asked Rianna.

We looked into the pit. Caliban was stuck in the filthy mud at the bottom, waving his hands over his head and bellowing ...

I recognised that movement at once. The hands waving above his head – even Caliban's animal shouts sounded familiar. I reached down to the monster's hair, grabbed a clammy handful ... and pulled it right off.

It wasn't hair – it was seaweed. The face hidden beneath it was very familiar too. My mouth fell open.

"Mr Fortune?!" I cried.

CHAPTER 7

Our Revels Are Now Ended

The monster in the pit wasn't Caliban – it was our missing headmaster, Mr Fortune. But he was in a terrible state. His face was red and puffy, his voice croaked and he was covered from head to toe in rank seaweed. No wonder he smelled like rotten fish.

"WHAT ARE YOU DOING?" he bellowed. "GET ME OUT OF HERE AT ONCE!"

We worked together to drag him out of the squelchy mud. He lay groaning on the sand.

The smell was so bad, it even woke Dom up again.

"Ooof, he STINKS!" said Dom, waving his hand over his face. "Why is he wearing all that gross seaweed?"

"And why is his voice so different?" said Ruby.

"And why does his face look like a smacked bottom?" asked Steve.

I leaned down to Mr Fortune. It was time for some answers. "Sir, what's going on? Where have you been?"

Mr Fortune looked up at us and began to tell his sorry tale.

"Uuuuurrrgghh ... what a day! After I fell out of the life raft, the waves washed me to a beach on the other side of the island. I took off my clothes and left them to dry in the sun ...

but then the tide came in and washed them away again! I ran into the water to try to get them back ... and stepped straight into a shoal of stinging jellyfish!"

We all winced. No wonder Mr Fortune looked like a burnt sausage. His skin was covered in a jellyfish sting rash!

"Then I remembered reading about seaweed being good for jellyfish stings," he groaned. "So I made myself a seaweed suit ... but the smell of fish attracted a flock of seagulls who started pecking me to ribbons! I ran into the forest in my bare feet to hide from them ... right into a patch of thorny thistles! My feet hurt so much that I tripped and fell forward ... right into a huge wasps' nest! I had a terrible allergic reaction to the wasp stings, which meant that my tongue and throat swelled up and I couldn't talk properly ..."

No wonder Steve hadn't recognised Mr Fortune's voice – the only sounds he could make with his swollen throat were monster roars.

"My day got worse and worse," continued Mr Fortune. "I managed to pull myself back to the beach to phone for help ... but someone had stolen my bag of phones! Finally, overcome with tiredness, I crawled into the forest and fell asleep. Then a few moments ago I heard voices nearby and woke up. It was Frank and Blake! I tried to speak to them, but something bumped into me and I fell straight into a cactus patch ..."

I patted Mr Fortune on the back. He didn't need to know that it was Rianna who had shoved him. The poor man had been through enough already.

"Well, that solves everything!" said Ruby. "There was no monster on the island – it was Mr Fortune all along!"

I frowned. She was wrong – there was lots that still needed explaining. "But ... what about the music in the trees? And the boxes of food that vanished? And the fact that everyone else is still missing?"

WHAM!

The beach around us suddenly lit up. We spun round. It took me a few seconds before I understood what was happening – the palm trees on the edge of the forest had floodlights hidden inside the leaves at the top, and now they were beaming down on us.

"*There* they are!" someone shouted from the trees.

I blinked into the light. I couldn't believe what I was seeing. A crowd of people were marching out of the forest towards us ... the rest of our drama club, safe and well! There was Leo and Tomi and Taylor and Petra, and all the others ... and there was someone else too. A tired-looking security guard in uniform, glaring down at us.

"What's going on here?" the guard shouted. "You kids have got a lot of explaining to do! Don't you know this park is private property?"

My head was reeling. "Park? What park?"

The guard turned around and pointed to the logo on the back of his jacket. It was a picture of a tropical island, with swirly writing underneath it:

I couldn't believe what I was reading. "This island is just a theme park?" I said.

"That's right!" said Leo, one of our classmates. "Our life raft landed in the harbour on the other side, just after the storm. That's where all the restaurants and hotels are!"

"We've spent all day waiting for your life raft to turn up," said Tomi. "We finally worked out what had happened when we saw Blake's message."

She held up her phone – it turned out that during the day, Blake had also found the time to post on social media. There was a picture of him posing in front of a dead jellyfish, with the caption *"stranded on a desert island lol"*.

"It got three likes!" said Blake. "Cool!"

Rianna shook her head. "But – what about the magical music in the trees? And what about the food that went missing ...?"

"Of course you heard music," said the security guard. "There are speakers hidden in every tree! We test the sound system every day to make sure it works properly." He glared at us. "And speaking of missing food ... I noticed someone had gone through those boxes I left out in the trees near our underground storage bunker! I hope someone's going to pay for that!"

Blake gulped and tried to hide behind me. I was too amazed to speak. The sandy beach, the tropical plants ... it was all fake. There was no magical storm, no enchanted island, no monster. We'd just accidentally washed up at a rubbish theme park.

"Right – enough talk!" said the security guard. "Who's in charge here?"

We pointed at Mr Fortune. He was snoring loudly on the sand, letting out the odd moan in his sleep. He definitely wasn't in charge at the moment.

"Oof," muttered the guard. "I'd better get him to a doctor. Who's next in charge?"

Dom stepped forward sheepishly – and pointed to me and Rianna.

"These two are," he said.

"That's right," said Ruby, wiping the warpaint off her face. "Frank and Rianna might not always be the loudest, but they *are* the most sensible."

Rianna and I grinned. The others were all nodding along. I couldn't believe it. Some things never change – but life can still surprise you.

"I guess everyone's pretty hungry," I said, turning to the security guard. "Can we get something to eat at one of those restaurants, please?"

He frowned suspiciously. "Do you have any money?"

"Not really," said Rianna. "But we could act out our play for you instead. Have you heard of *The Tempest?*"

The guard looked blank.

"We'll explain on the way," said Rianna. "Everyone remember their lines?"

The others cheered and followed her into the forest.

I stayed behind for a moment and stared up at the twinkling night sky. We might not have really been on a magical island, but something about tonight felt magic. All the stars were shining down on us – and not just the big ones either. You could see the tiny ones too, filling the gaps in between them. Out here, away from the mainland, they all shone just as brightly.

I caught up with Rianna and the two of us led the others away from the beach, into the Brave New World.

A Tropical Island

Watch out for Ross Montgomery's next Shakespeare-inspired tale of mishap and mayhem, this time inspired by *Macbeth*:

Our books are tested
for children and young people by
children and young people.

Thanks to everyone who consulted on
a manuscript for their time and effort in
helping us to make our books better
for our readers.